Princess Ponies 🐴

The Pumpkin Ghost

The Princess Ponies series

Princess Ponies

The Pumpkin Ghost

CHLOE RYDER

BLOOMSBURY
CHILDREN'S BOOKS
NEW YORK LONDON OXFORD NEW DELHI SYDNEY

BLOOMSBURY CHILDREN'S BOOKS
Bloomsbury Publishing Inc., part of Bloomsbury Publishing Plc
1385 Broadway, New York, NY 10018

BLOOMSBURY, BLOOMSBURY CHILDREN'S BOOKS, and the Diana logo are
trademarks of Bloomsbury Publishing Plc

First published in the United States of America in August 2019
by Bloomsbury Children's Books

Bloomsbury books may be purchased for business or promotional use. For information on
bulk purchases please contact Macmillan Corporate and Premium Sales Department at
specialmarkets@macmillan.com

Library of Congress Cataloging-in-Publication Data
available upon request
ISBN 978-1-5476-0166-0 (paperback) • ISBN 978-1-5476-0167-7 (e-book)

Printed and bound in China by Leo Paper Products, Heshan, Guangdong
2 4 6 8 10 9 7 5 3 1

All papers used by Bloomsbury Publishing Plc are natural, recyclable products
made from wood grown in well-managed forests. The manufacturing processes
conform to the environmental regulations of the country of origin.

To find out more about our authors and books visit www.bloomsbury.com
and sign up for our newsletters.

With special thanks to Julie Sykes

For Caden and Torin,
Happy Halloween!

The Pony

Queen
Moonshine

Princess
Crystal

Princess
Cloud

Princess
Stardust

Princess
Honey

Royal Family

King
Firestar

Prince
Jet

Prince
Comet

Prince
Storm

Chevalia

Prologue

Hidden in the middle of the seas, and surrounded by golden beaches, is the magical island of Chevalia. The island is ruled by the royal ponies Queen Moonshine and King Firestar from their court at Stableside Castle.

But a long way from Stableside, in the middle of the Horseshoe Hills, was a smaller, dilapidated castle with crumbling, ivy-clad walls. Mice and beetles scurried through the empty rooms. Bats roosted in the turrets and spiders hung from thick webs.

At the back of the castle, in a damp, dark room, a mean-looking pony with a square nose was getting ready to go out. She took her time, using a comb to arrange her mane so that it fell over her chestnut forehead and neck. Afterward, she carefully painted her hooves with sparkly black hoof polish.

"How do I look?" she wondered aloud. She turned to a broken mirror and looked at herself. With a huge smile, she nodded at her reflection.

"As good as my name! I look *divine*!" Divine's voice rose as she continued to speak to her reflection. "Royal ponies, you lead perfect lives in your precious castle, but not for much longer! Enjoy

the luxury of Stableside while you can. Soon, with a little help from my new and spooky servants, you'll be desperate to leave. When you are gone, the royal jewels will be mine and I will crown myself the new queen of Chevalia."

Chapter 1

Pippa MacDonald opened the front door and stepped outside. "Look at the moon," she said. "It's huge."

A large harvest moon hung over the houses across the street. It even had an orange hue, just like a pumpkin.

"It's a good night for trick-or-treating," said her mom with a smile. She carried a plastic jack-o'-lantern with a flickering light inside.

Pippa's little brother, Jack, dressed as a skeleton, pushed past Mom to gape at the moon.

"Don't push, Jack," said Mom. "We're not going to leave without you. Hurry up, Miranda. Your makeup looks fine."

Pippa adjusted her Halloween costume, a gray pony onesie with yellow eyes. "What do you think of my zombie pony costume?"

"You look like a real zony," said her mom with a grin.

"I think you look scary," said Jack. "So do you, Miranda."

Pippa's big sister wore a long, flowing black gown with a witch's hat on her head.

"Ugh," she grunted. "I'm not trying

to be scary. I'm going for glamorous! And I'd much rather go trick-or-treating with my friends instead of my family."

"You all look great," said Mom. "And we always do Halloween as a family. It's our tradition."

"Well, maybe traditions should change," said Miranda.

Pippa didn't want anything to

change, but she didn't want to go out with her grumpy sister either. "Maybe you should stay home," she said.

"Kids," said Mom, "that's enough. Miranda, Pippa, we stick together."

"So long as there's candy," shouted Jack, running to the sidewalk.

"Jack, wait!" Pippa pretended she was a zony, galloping after him with a weird, jerky gait.

"No way!" shrieked Jack. "You can't catch me. I'm going to eat all the candy!" He raced around the corner of the street, then stopped suddenly. His voice dropped to a whisper. "Look at that old house. It's real spooky at night."

"That's because it's haunted," said Miranda, catching up. "Mrs. Parsons, the old lady who lives there, is a real witch! Bet you won't knock on her door, Pippa. You're too much of a baby."

"I am not," said Pippa. She didn't know why Miranda was always so mean to her. She hadn't always been like this, but ever since Miranda started middle school, she'd begun acting so superior. Pippa clutched her pumpkin-shaped bucket. "We should start at this end of the street first. We'll knock at the haunted house last."

Secretly, Pippa was scared. She didn't really believe in ghosts and witches, but the old house was covered in ivy and surrounded by thick bushes. It was dark and uninviting, the sort of place where ghosts would hang out, if there really were ghosts. Pippa hoped that by the time they reached the end of the street, their buckets would be so full of candy that they'd have to go home without knocking there.

"Pippa's a silly baby," said Miranda. "I don't want to trick-or-treat with her."

Pippa opened her mouth to argue, but Miranda walked off with Jack. Pippa was about to follow when she heard someone call her name. The sound came from the direction of the old house. Her pulse sped up.

"Pippa!"

Pippa squeaked with fright. Could the house really be haunted? But how would the ghost know her name?

"Pippa!"

A draft of air caught Pippa's wavy brown hair, sweeping it over her face. She looked up as she pushed it away.

A silver-gray pony with a long mane and tail was hovering in the air.

"Cloud!" Pippa's voice rose with astonishment and relief. "What are you doing here?"

"I came to see you, Pippa MacDonald." Cloud dropped lower until she could whisper in Pippa's ear. "Chevalia needs your help. Princess Stardust was

too frightened to come with me. She sent a message instead, asking you to come *immediately*."

Pippa was alarmed. "What's happened? Is Stardust all right?"

"No time for that now," Cloud answered. "I'll tell you on the way."

Pippa glanced at her family. Jack and Miranda were arguing, and her hassled-looking mother was trying to make peace.

"You won't be missed. Remember that time stops in your world when you visit Chevalia. Please, Pippa?"

"Of course," said Pippa. She'd never ignore a cry for help from her best pony friend, Princess Stardust. "How will I get there? Shall I ride on your back?"

Cloud chuckled. "I've got a better

idea." Swooping down, she hovered in front of Pippa. Cloud had a magical power. She could make ponies fly by rubbing her nose against theirs. "I'm loving your outfit; are you a zony?"

"Yes!" Pippa was delighted that Cloud had guessed.

Cloud rubbed Pippa's nose with hers. There was a sudden loud, ripping noise.

"Oh no! I've torn my outfit." Pippa turned her head. Out of the corner of her eye, she saw two slits opening. "Wings!" she gasped. Two enormous feathery wings were sprouting in the region of her shoulder blades. Pippa gasped as she rose in the air a little way. "Thanks, Cloud, but I'm not a real pony, so can I fly with them?"

"Of course," said Cloud. "Your wings will last until your feet touch the ground. Hurry, Pippa, there's no time to lose."

Pippa moved into the shadows cast by a large bush and tested her wings. They felt stiff and were difficult to move. She dropped her candy bucket on the ground so she could put all her effort into flying. That was better. Once she concentrated, the wings moved easily. Pippa made them flap with a large sweeping movement. "Look, Cloud!" she squeaked excitedly as she rose higher. "I'm flying."

She glanced down at her family, half hoping they'd see her, but they were frozen in time and looked like statues, Jack and Miranda in mid-argument over who should carry the jack-o'-lantern and Mom exasperated, running a hand through her hair.

"You're a natural," called Cloud encouragingly. "But don't flap so fast! That's better. Now, follow me."

Pippa moved her wings in the same rhythm as Cloud. Flying was the most exciting thing ever—after discovering Chevalia, of course!

Pippa called softly down to Mom, Miranda, and Jack, "I'll be back before you know it."

She flapped her wings and chased after Cloud with a cry of, "To Chevalia!"

Chapter 2

Side by side, Pippa and Cloud flew out to sea. It was a clear night, and the dark sky was lit with a smattering of stars and the huge pumpkin moon. Beneath her, Pippa caught glimpses of trick-or-treating children frozen in time, dressed as witches, ghosts, zombies, and skeletons.

"Do you have Halloween in Chevalia?" Pippa asked Cloud.

Cloud sighed. "Yes, we do. It was

one of the traditions that the ponies who
left the human world to live in Chevalia
wanted to keep. Halloween is great fun.
The foals go around the island in costume
trick-or-treating for chocolate-covered
carrots and toasted oats. There's a prize
for the scariest pony and one for the best
jack-o'-lantern. We finish with a feast at
Stableside Castle—only not this year."

"Why not?"

"Something terrible has happened. That's why Stardust sent for you." Cloud's voice trembled with disbelief as she continued, "Stableside Castle is haunted."

"No way!" breathed Pippa.

"That's what I thought. Queen Moonshine refused to believe it too. At first, she put all the ghostly noises down to trick-or-treaters getting in some early practice. But as Halloween approached, the haunting became more terrifying until . . ." Cloud broke off with a shudder. "But we're almost here. Stardust can tell you the rest."

Flying was hot work, especially dressed in a zony onesie, but Pippa felt a chill run through her. If Stableside

Castle really was haunted, what was she supposed to do about it?

"Cloud . . ." Pippa wanted to go home but she couldn't find the courage to say so.

Cloud must have guessed her anxiety. "Pippa MacDonald," she said softly, "you're the girl who's saved Chevalia not once, but many times. You are the bravest girl in pony history. Believe in yourself, and others will rally around you."

Pippa swallowed. What was more terrifying: facing a haunted castle, or failing her friends? But of course there was only one answer.

"Thanks, Cloud," she said. "I'll do my best."

As Chevalia came into sight, Cloud swooped down over its golden beaches bathed in the late afternoon sun. Pippa followed, her hooves skimming the tops of the trees in the Forbidden Forest, until Mane Street came into view at the far end of the grassy plateau.

Pippa's mouth dropped open and she almost forgot to fly at the sight that greeted her. At the farthest end of Mane Street, right opposite the fairground, there was a brightly-colored village of tents.

"What's that?" she asked, as Cloud flew closer.

"A new, temporary, Stableside Castle," said Cloud. "The ponies of Chevalia have been very generous. The royal family and court left in a great hurry, without taking any of their belongings. All day, the other ponies have been arriving with tents, bedding, cooking equipment, and just about everything a royal pony on an impromptu camping trip could need."

"That's what I love about Chevalia," said Pippa, gliding to the ground and landing a few hoof spaces from Cloud on a patch of empty grass. There was a soft pop and her wings disappeared. "Look! There's Princess Stardust."

Pippa's shoulders felt stiff from flying and she lurched toward her friend.

Princess Stardust's eyes widened. With a panicked snort she backed away.

"Stardust?" Pippa was confused until she suddenly remembered that she was wearing her zony outfit. Laughing, she pulled off her hood to reveal herself. "It's me, Pippa. Stardust, wait!"

"Pippa?" Stardust's hooves skidded in the grass as she stopped running. She stared at Pippa for a full minute; then her eyes blazed with fury. "That isn't funny! You shouldn't scare ponies like that!"

"But . . . I didn't mean to scare you. I was trick-or-treating when Cloud came to get me. I forgot that I'm dressed as a zony."

A rosy blush tinged Stardust's white coat. "You didn't scare *me*!" she said haughtily. "I was worried that you might scare the little ponies. Of course I knew it was you."

Pippa hid a smile. "What do you think of my outfit? It's cool, isn't it?"

"It's quite nice," said Stardust, sounding less grumpy. She looked Pippa up and down. "I might dress up as a zony next year."

Pippa smiled. "That'd be fun," she said. "I missed you, Stardust. I'm glad I'm here."

"I missed you too." Stardust nuzzled Pippa's hair. "It's horrible here now. We're living in tents. There's no room to swing a tail. I've got to share with Princess Crystal and Princess Honey. They keep sending me on errands and treating me like a baby just because I'm younger than them."

"Living in a tent village looks like fun," said Pippa. "Can I have a look?"

"Fun?" Stardust seemed put out. "I suppose you can look, if you're sure you want to."

Stardust led Pippa into the first tent.

It smelled of crushed grass and was almost as cold inside as out. "This is our new dining room," said Stardust, her nose wrinkling in distaste.

The makeshift dining room was dirty and nowhere near as luxurious as the grand dining hall at Stableside Castle, where the ponies ate from ornate feeding troughs and crystal chandeliers hung

from the ceiling. Pippa took in the two low wooden benches with buckets arranged in a line on top. They'd clearly been made in a hurry. "I love the decorations," she said, in an effort to say something nice. She pointed at the paper flags covered with tiny horseshoes that hung from the tent poles.

"You wait until you see my bedroom," sniffed Stardust. "It's yucky." She went toward a door at the back of the dining tent just as another pony came the other way.

"Queen Moonshine." Pippa and Stardust dropped curtsies.

"Welcome back, Pippa MacDonald." Queen Moonshine dipped her head regally. Her long white mane trailed on the muddy ground and her hooves were splattered with dirt. "Thank you for coming to our rescue once again. As you can see, something awful has happened. We've been forced to abandon Stableside Castle because it's haunted by a ghost. At first, I didn't believe it. But it's true. The royal family evacuated to these terrible conditions. But one does what one must when facing a haunting."

"I guess so," agreed Pippa.

Queen Moonshine dropped her head and looked straight at Pippa. "You are the bravest soul I know. Would you investigate the haunted castle for me? For Chevalia?"

Pippa shoved her hands inside the pockets of her onesie so that Queen Moonshine wouldn't see how much they were trembling.

25

Could there be *real* ghosts in Chevalia? The idea was terrifying. And she could see that the Queen was scared, scared enough to move her entire family out of the castle. Pippa took a deep breath and said, "Yes, your majesty. I will investigate." And then she added, "If Stardust comes with me."

"Me!" squeaked Stardust. "What use would I be? I'm the youngest!"

"But you're not a baby," said Pippa. "You're the bravest pony ever. Remember when we were looking for the missing gold horseshoes? You thought the Cloud Forest was haunted, but you still searched it with me. Please, Princess Stardust. We can face anything if we do it together."

There was a long silence.

26

"Okay," said Stardust, quietly. "I'll come."

"Thank you, my friend!" Pippa threw her arms round Stardust and hugged her.

Word soon spread around the tent village that Pippa and Stardust were going to investigate the castle ghost. When they left for Stableside, the royal ponies gathered to cheer for them. Pippa walked faster and stood taller; the cheers made her feel better.

Eventually they left the tents far behind them and approached Stableside Castle.

"It's so quiet," said Stardust as they neared the castle walls.

"That's because there's no one here," said Pippa. Her palms were sweaty with fear. She rubbed them on her costume, trying to be brave. But, what would they find when they entered the castle?

But they didn't get that far. As they approached the drawbridge, a long moan rippled across the moat. Stardust almost jumped into Pippa's arms.

"What was that?" she croaked.

"I don't know!" said Pippa, gripping Stardust.

The moan grew louder.

"Stardust," whispered Pippa, nervously looking around, "it's getting closer!"

"Aaaarghh!" Stardust jumped back, her body trembling. She screamed so loud it almost drowned out the ghostly moans.

A milk-white pony appeared high on the castle wall.

Pippa felt hot and cold at the same time. In disbelief, she watched the ghostly pony rear up, slashing its hooves above its horrible head. Not a pony head, but a fiery orange pumpkin with a gaping mouth and slits for eyes.

They had found the ghost.

Chapter 3

Stardust let out a shrill whinny. "Run!" she cried. Stardust spun around and galloped back toward the safety of Mane Street.

"Stardust, wait!" Pippa called. She wished she still had wings as she ran after the princess pony.

Pippa's lungs stung with exertion as she finally caught Stardust by grabbing at her white tail.

"Aaagh! Get off me, Pumpkin Ghost!" screamed Stardust.

"It's only me," Pippa said. "Your friend, Pippa."

Stardust stopped so suddenly Pippa smacked into her. Pushing Stardust's tail out of her face, Pippa kept talking. "What's wrong? We've faced far scarier things than this before. Remember the time Cloud gave you wings, and we flew into the heart of the volcano to rescue the last golden horseshoe? That was terrifying."

"It wasn't as frightening as the Pumpkin Ghost," whispered Stardust, her hooves trembling.

"I don't think it is a ghost."

"What is it, then?"

Pippa pulled the hood of the zony costume back over her head and moaned. Stardust shivered, and Pippa laughed.

"A pony in a costume," said Pippa, removing the hood again.

"Do you think so?" asked Stardust.

Pippa nodded with certainty. "That ghost was too solid-looking. I think it's a pony wearing a giant pumpkin on its head. I wonder . . . Stardust, can you think of anywhere on the island that has pumpkins big enough to wear?"

Stardust shook her head. "I can't."

"What about Mucker?" Pippa asked, suddenly remembering Stardust's friend who farmed the grasslands. "He might know."

"That's a smashing idea," said Stardust.

"Jump on my back and we'll go and ask him."

"Thanks!" It had been a long time since Pippa had ridden Stardust. Grasping a handful of mane, she vaulted onto her back.

"Yay!" Stardust whinnied, happier now that Pippa was riding on her back. "Let's go." She set off at a fast canter.

Pippa sat tall, letting her body move to the same rhythm as Stardust's. It was exhilarating to see the ground flashing past and feel the wind lifting her wavy brown hair. Best of all, Pippa loved it when Stardust jumped over obstacles: a rotting tree trunk, a stream, and once a large boulder. It felt like flying, but without having to flap any wings. Pippa sat forward, her hands sliding up

Stardust's neck to make the jump easier for her friend.

All too soon, they reached the Grass-land.

"Look, there's Mucker," snorted Stardust.

Pippa scanned the field full of golden straw bales and saw a stocky pony with a white blaze and four white stockings adorning his dark brown coat.

"Trick or treat, Mucker!" she called.

Mucker dropped the straw bale he was lifting onto a trailer and leaned against it. "Pippa and Stardust!" he whinnied in delight. "It would be a treat if you've come to help me bring the harvest in."

Pippa loved helping out on Mucker's farm. "Actually," she started, "we've

come to ask you a question about a ghost."

"Not *the* ghost!" Mucker's eyes were enormous. Slowly he lifted another straw bale onto the trailer. "Now, that's a story!"

"Tell us," begged Stardust. "Please, Mucker."

"Of course, but after I've got the

straw in." Mucker nodded at the sky. "It's getting late and it looks like rain."

Pippa looked up. The sun was low in the sky, and dark rain clouds were gathering overhead. "We'll help you," she said.

"Great call," said Stardust. Quietly she added, "I'd much rather be farming with Mucker than hunting a pumpkin ghost."

Mucker was pleased and told Pippa and Stardust to bring the straw bales to the trailer so that he could load them. With three of them working together, it wasn't long before all the straw was safely under cover in the big barn.

"Phew," said Pippa, wiping her forehead and leaving a smear of dirt there. "That was fun, but very hard work."

"Good job," said Mucker. "Come back to the farmhouse for a trough of hot apple juice."

Stardust looked at Pippa longingly. "Mucker makes the best apple juice around."

Pippa hesitated. Hot apple juice was very tempting, but the sun was setting and Queen Moonshine had trusted her with an important job. "Next time we visit," she said. "Hopefully by then, we'll have caught our ghost."

"Ghosts." Mucker's dark brown face paled. "I've not told anyone this before, except for my farming friends, but our fields are haunted too! Every night, when the sun goes down, a ghost appears. It makes horrid noises— moans and whooshing sounds, which grow louder as it comes closer. Anyone unlucky enough to be caught out in the fields has to duck for cover. But mostly there's no one brave enough to go out at night."

"Really?" Pippa gave Mucker a suspicious look. Was he teasing them? "So have you actually seen this ghost?"

Mucker shook his head.

"What about pumpkins?" Pippa continued. "Do any of your farmer friends grow giant ones, let's say the size of a pony's head?"

"Pumpkins! What's that got to do with ghosts?"

"The scourge of Stableside Castle wears a pumpkin on its head," chipped in Stardust.

"Really!" exclaimed Mucker. "Well,

the Ponykin Patch Farm grows the biggest pumpkins in Chevalia. Do you want me to show you where it is?"

"Yes, please," Pippa and Stardust chorused.

"Let me lock up first." Mucker plodded around the farm, padlocking the barns and shutting up the geese. Pippa silently urged him to hurry as she and Stardust followed him. At last the farm and the outbuildings were secure, but by then the sun had almost set.

"We'd better hurry," said Mucker, nervously checking over his shoulder.

Pippa took a deep breath and managed not to tell Mucker that he was the one holding everyone up.

The fields were prickly with corn

stubble that crackled under feet and hooves. Pippa and her pony friends were halfway across when Stardust pulled up, ears twitching.

"What's that?"

Across the field came a low whisper that was growing into something much louder.

"Whoooooooooooo."

Pippa felt the blood rush from her face. "Eeek!" she squealed. Why hadn't she believed Mucker's story? "It's a . . ."

Stardust tucked her head into Pippa's embrace; the rest of her sentence buried in her soft white mane.

"Aaaaargh!" Mucker yelped, jumping in the air. "It's the ghost! Run!"

Chapter 4

The ghost pony drifted closer.

"Gallop!" squealed Stardust.

Clouds of straw dust rose in the air as she pounded across the field with Mucker by her side. Pippa held on for her life, bouncing up and down on Stardust's back.

"Whooooooo!"

The sky was full of racing dark clouds. But what was that? Pippa saw a pale shape slide between the clouds.

"The ghost!" she shouted. "Faster, Stardust!"

"Can't!" puffed Stardust, her hoof steps faltering.

"You can!" Mucker ran by her side, urging her on. "See that building there, across the field? It's not far, and we can shelter there."

Stardust galloped toward the building, finally outpacing the ghost.

"What is this place?" called Pippa as the building came closer. A wooden sign with a picture of a lamb on ice skates swung from a tall pole. "Mucker!" Pippa gave a shaky laugh. "Have you brought us to an inn?"

"The Skating Lamb," panted Mucker, slowing as he navigated the gate, which was topped with a row of tiny jack-o'-lanterns, their candles flickering in the breeze. "They serve the best carrot juice for miles."

Pippa slid from Stardust's back and pushed open the door. A fug of warm air and chatter spilled into the cold night.

"Come in quick and shut the door," called a tiny black pony. Her big eyes sparkled as brightly as the green emeralds decorating her mane. She stood behind a counter, pouring something orange into a pint-sized drinking trough. "Mucker! Good to see you, darlin'. I'd offer you the usual, but we're serving our special Halloween menu tonight. Hot pumpkin juice instead?"

"Yes, please, Nell, hot pumpkin juice for three," said Mucker.

Pippa stared curiously around the

room. It was packed with ponies of all sizes. In the corner, several ponies with troughs of pumpkin juice were arguing amicably over a game of horseshoes. One pony was tossing pony nuts in the air for another to catch in his mouth. Lots of ponies were eating from wooden troughs. The walls were hung with horse brasses, polished so that they reflected like tiny mirrors, and plates with pictures of horses' heads.

"Look, Stardust! It's your family."

Stardust stared at the plates, each one displaying the portrait of a different member of her royal family. Her face turned pink. Looking away quickly, she said, "Mmmmm, can you smell that? Pumpkin pie and bran mash."

"There you go," said Nell, slapping three steaming troughs of pumpkin juice down. Suddenly she froze. Leaning forward, she peered at Stardust. Her eyes widened. "Princess Stardust! I thought I recognized you. How remark-able! Princess Stardust with Pippa MacDonald, the brave girl." Nell curt-sied. "What brings you both to my humble inn?"

"A ghost," said Stardust.

Nell paled. "You saw the ghost? You poor wee things. Well, you're safe now. Here at the Skating Lamb, we hear the ghost all the time but it's never dared to venture inside."

"It's really lovely in here," said Stardust. "I wish we could stay the night."

"Well, you can." Nell curtsied again. "We have bedrooms fit for a queen. Or a princess," she added.

"You have rooms?" Stardust's eyes lit up. "I'm too scared to go back outside."

Pippa shook her head, guessing that Stardust was also looking for an excuse not to spend another night in the royal tent. The more she thought about it, the angrier it made her. Poor Stardust! She and her family had been forced out of their home. As her anger rose, Pippa could hardly stand still. When Nell offered to show Stardust the guest rooms, Pippa slipped outside.

The night was freezing after the warmth of the inn. Pippa wrapped her trembling arms around her chest and tried to convince herself it was only the chilly night air that was making her shiver. She pulled the zony hood over her head to keep warm.

She walked as far as the gate and stopped. Her feet felt heavy, but she couldn't give up now. Ghosts didn't exist. They were made up to scare people. Bravely lifting her chin, Pippa opened the gate and walked into the fields.

A low moan rippled toward her on

the breeze. Pippa's heart thudded loudly. Her instinct was to run, but scrunching her hands into fists she stood her ground.

"Whoooooo," called the ghost.

"Whooooo," Pippa called back.

"WHOOOOOO."

"WHOOOOOOOOO!" yelled Pippa.

"AAAARRRRRRGH."

"WHOOOOOOOO, AAAAARRR-RRGH," Pippa wailed into the night, even though she was terrified.

Something flew low over Pippa's head. The draft blew her hair in her eyes. Pushing it back, she glared into the darkness. The ghost let out a shriek that sounded as if it were actually scared.

"Agh! A zombie pony," it cried in a voice that was familiar to Pippa.

"Cloud, is that you?" Pippa asked, pulling her hood off.

"It's you, Pippa!" Cloud cried from above.

Pippa stared at the silver-gray pony now hovering in front of her. Crossly she asked, "What are you doing here? Why are you pretending to be a ghost?"

"Ghost? Me? No!" Cloud was shocked. "Is that what you thought? I'm so sorry, Pippa. I didn't mean to scare you. It's what I do every night to frighten the mice and stop them from nibbling the crops. I'm being a flying scarehorse."

"Like a scarecrow." Pippa laughed. "You are a scarehorse all right! Everyone thinks the fields are haunted."

"Really?" Now Cloud was laughing

51

too. "And in the darkness, I thought you were a real zony!"

"Pippa! Are you all right?" The inn door burst open. Stardust, Mucker, Nell, and everyone from the Skating Lamb piled outside.

"Cloud," said Stardust, "did you save Pippa from the ghost?"

Cloud was laughing so hard she could barely keep her hooves off the ground. "You tell them, Pippa," she chuckled. "I need all my strength to stop from landing."

"Don't do that!" Pippa launched into an explanation before a disaster happened and Cloud touched down. Then her flying magic would be lost forever.

Pippa explained that, far from scaring the farmers, Cloud had been trying to help them. Soon everyone was laughing so much they ended up crying.

"Thanks, Cloud." Nell wiped a tear from her eye. "I hope we haven't put you off doing such an important job."

"Not at all," said Cloud. She was back in control of herself and hovering at head height. "I love my nighttime routine. But I wouldn't mind a trough of hot carrot juice now and then. It smells amazing. I'm a little hurt that no one ever thought to bring me some, when I've been working so hard to help you all."

"You can have as much carrot juice as you like," said Nell, stamping her hoof on the ground. "It'll be my pleasure."

"There," said Pippa. "One mystery solved. Things aren't always what they seem."

"Yes," said Stardust thoughtfully. "Nell, if you don't mind, I won't stay the night here after all. I'll come back another time and bring my family. But right now, Pippa and I have another mystery to solve. Mucker, where are those giant pumpkins?"

"Ponykin Patch," said Mucker. "It's not far. Let's go there now."

Chapter 5

Ponykin Patch Farm was tucked away in a hollow between the Grasslands and the Savannah. The old farmhouse had a thatched roof and roses growing over the door. In the corner stood a tall barn with wooden doors, secured by a large padlock. It was covered in pretend flying bats, and fake giant furry spiders dangled from cobwebs. An orange post-and-rail fence surrounded the buildings.

Hanging from it were hundreds of jack-o'-lanterns.

"It's so pretty!" exclaimed Pippa.

"Spooky, too!" said Stardust, walking slower.

"There's the pumpkin patch," said Mucker. He pointed with a hoof.

"Wow!" Pippa had never seen such enormous pumpkins. "I'd love one of

those! It would be great for trick-or-treat."

"They're huge!" Stardust agreed.

"Think of all the pumpkin soup and pie you could make," said Mucker wistfully.

"Can I help you?" The farmhouse door opened and a muscular black-and-white cart horse stepped outside. Her face was rosy, and her black mane and tail were plaited through with straw.

"Who's there, Marrow?" An older cart horse with similar black-and-white markings came to the door. "What do you want, this time of the night?"

Pippa quickly explained that they were looking for the biggest pumpkins in Chevalia, ones that could be worn on a pony's head.

"Then you've come to the right place. I'm Farmer Squash and this is my daughter, Marrow. Our largest pumpkins are so enormous a pony could easily wear one on his head."

"Really?" Pippa and Stardust exchanged an excited look. "Could we see them?"

Farmer Squash shook his head. "Much as I'd like to show you, they're locked away. We're keeping them for the Biggest Pumpkin competition at this year's Harvest Fair."

Marrow nudged her father and whispered something in his ear.

"Who?" he said loudly. "*Really?*"

He looked at Stardust and Pippa again. "But of course I'll make an exception for *you*."

Sidestepping the flickering jack-o'-lanterns decorating the yard, everyone trooped over to the barn. Pippa took a deep breath, enjoying the familiar smell of smoke, candle wax, and warm pumpkin, as Marrow unlocked the barn with an iron key hung round her neck on an orange ribbon.

"There you go," said Farmer Squash as the barn door creaked open.

Pippa, Stardust, and Mucker peered inside expectantly. The barn was completely empty.

"What!" gasped Farmer Squash. "Where are my prize pumpkins?"

Pippa had an idea. Grimly she asked, "Who else has a key to the barn?"

"Only us," said Marrow. "Oh, and our two stable hooves, Hairy and Lanky."

"Are they here now?" asked Stardust.

"They left this afternoon," said Farmer Squash. "They wanted to go home to celebrate Halloween and the Harvest Fair next week with their families."

Princess Stardust sighed heavily. "We're too late."

But Pippa was not going to give up so easily. She'd promised Queen

Moonshine that she'd investigate the pumpkin ghost, and she wouldn't stop until she had exhausted every lead.

"Where did Hairy and Lanky sleep when they were working here?" Pippa asked.

"In the stables behind the barn," said Marrow. "Would you like to see them?"

It was dark behind the barn. Pippa picked up a jack-o'-lantern to shine some light on the stables as they went inside. "There's nothing here," said Stardust, pawing the straw on the ground.

"Keep looking." Pippa slowly made her way around the room. She wrinkled her nose. It smelled of sour apples and damp hay.

"What's that?" Pippa sprang at the nearly empty hay net dangling from the wall. Sticking out of the string mesh was a piece of paper. She put her hand inside the net and pulled it out.

"A newspaper." Stardust was disappointed.

"*Chevalia Now*," read Pippa. "It's an old copy." She opened it up. "Ooh, look, Stardust. There's a piece on the royal family."

"There always is," said Stardust, rolling her eyes.

Pippa scanned the column. "It's about the castle jewels, and there's a great picture. Hairy and Lanky obviously enjoyed reading this. They've marked the article with a horseshoe print . . ." Pippa's voice trailed away. "Stardust," she asked, "where are the royal jewels now?"

"Where they always are—on display

in the jewel room at Stableside Castle," Stardust replied.

"But no one's there, unless you left some guards behind."

"Of course we didn't. Everyone was too scared to stay. You saw how terrible the pumpkin ghost was." Stardust stared at Pippa in dismay as she realized what Pippa was thinking. "Oh no! Hairy and Lanky are planning to steal them, aren't they?"

"Yes!" said Pippa. "But don't worry. I've got a plan. Farmer Squash, could we have three pumpkins big enough for Stardust, Mucker, and me to wear on our heads?"

Farmer Squash looked at Pippa as if she were crazy. "They may not be prizewinners, but of course," he said.

"Though I've no idea why you'd want to do that."

"To scare some ghosts!" said Pippa, with a grin.

While Pippa carved three pumpkins into jack-o'-lanterns, Stardust explained how Stableside Castle had suddenly become haunted.

"So it was all a ruse. You think that Hairy and Lanky are going to steal the castle jewels?" asked Marrow.

"Exactly!" Pippa put down her carving tool and placed a pumpkin on Stardust's head. "Oooh, that's really scary." She giggled as Stardust let out a low moan.

Mucker looked just as frightening with his pumpkin head, and everyone assured Pippa that she was terrifying too. Marrow rushed into the farmhouse and came out with three large white sheets.

"To complete the outfit," she said, draping them over the three friends.

With lots of howls and moans, Pippa, Stardust, and Mucker said goodbye to Farmer Squash and Marrow. It was a long, dark ride back to Mane Street, lit only by the stars.

"This is such fun!" said Pippa, as they rode down Mane Street toward the royal camp.

"Whoooo!" Stardust agreed.

"Aaaargh!" shrieked Dolly, a dumpy gray pony who was locking up her café, Dolly's Tea Rooms, for the night. "It's the pumpkin ghosts!"

"Wait, Dolly, don't run away. It's

only us." Pippa snatched off her pumpkin head and waved it at Miss Dolly.

"Pippa MacDonald! Fancy tricking me like that." Dolly burst out laughing. "But what a scare you all gave me! Here, have some candied carrots."

"Thanks," said Pippa, shoving the carrots in her pocket to share with Stardust and Mucker later.

Pippa popped her pumpkin head back on as they rode toward the royal tents. Comet was wandering from one tent to another, a jack-o'-lantern around his neck.

"D-d-d-don't harm me . . . p-p-please," he said, backing away when he saw Pippa and her friends.

"Eeeeek!" screamed Princess Honey,

coming out of another tent. "Mom! Save me!"

"Honey, darling, what's up?" Queen Moonshine came galloping, her tail flying out behind her.

"It's only us!" Pippa revealed herself quickly. "Don't be frightened. We didn't mean to scare you. We came to tell you that we're going to catch the ghosts at Stableside Castle."

Chapter 6

With cries of "Good luck!" and "Be careful!" ringing in their ears, Pippa, Stardust, and Mucker rode up to Stableside Castle.

"We'll use the secret way in," said Stardust, heading along a narrow path that led downhill.

Pippa remembered using the small door hidden in the castle walls on her first-ever visit to Chevalia, when she and Stardust had wanted to avoid being photographed by the ponarazzi. The hidden door opened into a huge court-yard with a stone wall at one end. Pippa was relieved to see the eight golden horseshoes safely glimmering on the wall. Chevalia needed its golden horse-shoes to survive. Thank goodness the thieves hadn't been foolish enough to try to steal them too.

Stardust led the way through a series of corridors to the jewel room. Mucker followed slowly behind, muttering, "This is all wrong. I've never been allowed this far inside the castle before."

"What's that?" Stardust drew up suddenly, her ears swivelling. From the cellars came the faint sound of scratch-ing. "Aaargh! It's the pumpkin ghosts!"

"Run!" said Mucker.

"Wait! The ghosts aren't real," Pippa said, trying to reassure the farmer pony. "That's Hairy and Lanky dressed up like ghosts to frighten everyone!"

"Of course! It's so spooky being here alone that I forgot." Stardust started forward again, not stopping until she reached the jewel room. She nudged open the door and trotted inside. A glass display case lined with pink silk dominated the room. Smaller display cases encircled it, lined with pale pink silk and lit with flaming torches. Pippa gasped and Stardust let out a sob. The doors were open. Every single display case was empty. The thieves had taken the jewels, and in their place they'd left two of the biggest jack-o'-lanterns Pippa had ever seen.

Angrily, Mucker stamped a hoof. "Those villains!" he snorted.

"We're too late," sniffed Stardust.

"Maybe not," Pippa said, holding up a hand. "Can you hear that?"

"Scratching," said Stardust. "And is that the sound of hoof steps? Do you think that's Hairy and Lanky?"

"Only one way to find out," said Pippa gallantly. "Let's go."

Stardust led the way, following the scratching down toward the cellars. "This feels all wrong," she whispered. "There's no way out down here."

"Good," said Pippa. "Then we'll catch the thieves red-hoofed."

But as they reached the bottom of the last staircase, they found the way to the dungeons blocked by a pile of earth.

Pippa stared into a newly dug hole in the wall. A tunnel snaked away from her. It was dark and uninviting and smelled like a sewer. Taking a deep breath, she said bravely, "This is how they got out. Quick, let's go after them!"

Pippa had to hunch her shoulders to stop her jack-o'-lantern head from bumping against the low ceiling. Stardust and Mucker stumbled along, their hoof steps muffled. Suddenly, Pippa caught sight of something ahead. Two ponies were creeping through the tunnels.

"Er, Hairy, I think there's something following us," called the end one nervously.

"Don't be silly, Lanky. How can there be when we scared them all away?"

Lanky turned around and saw the pumpkin ghosts following him. He opened his mouth and screamed so loudly that he almost dropped the sack he was carrying. "Waaaaaaaa! Pumpkin ghosts. Real live pumpkin ghosts!"

Hairy looked back and, with an even louder scream than Lanky's, he took off.

"After them!" said Pippa.

Pippa climbed onto Stardust's back. Stardust broke into a gallop, Mucker following close behind.

"Go, Stardust," urged Pippa, leaning forward as she shouted encouragement to her friend.

It was one of the most frightening and most exhilarating rides of Pippa's life. As they galloped along the freshly dug tunnel, the ground shook and earth fell from the ceiling. It showered them with small stones and the occasional worm.

"We'll never get out alive," panted Stardust, after she'd galloped for ages. "There isn't an end."

"There has to be," yelled Pippa. "Keep going, Stardust. It can't be far now!" She picked a worm from Stardust's mane and dropped it on the ground.

"I can see light!" Stardust panted at last. Finding an extra burst of energy, she galloped toward it. Mucker thundered on behind her.

"Where are we?" Pippa stared around as Stardust burst out of the tunnel's end. "This is the Wild Forest. Have we really come that far?"

"Looks like it!" Stardust was just as amazed as Pippa. She slowed to a canter, then a trot, and finally stopped. Mucker pulled up behind her, snorting. His sides heaved as he fought for breath.

"Where did Hairy and Lanky go?" Pippa sat forward, straining her ears for sounds of the two thieves.

The forest seemed even darker than the tunnel. The hair on the back of Pippa's neck rose as she listened to the spooky rustles and squeaks of the unseen creatures rooting around in the trees. Suddenly a wicked cackle rang out.

"Who's that?" Pippa thought she recognized the voice, which sent goose-bumps running up her arms. If only she could remember why!

Then Pippa, Stardust, and Mucker all remembered at the same time. "*Divine!*" they whispered.

Chapter 7

On the tips of their hooves, Stardust, with Pippa on her back, and Mucker crept toward Divine. After a while, the trees thinned and gave way to a small clearing with a thatched cottage. Poison ivy grew up the walls, and on either side of the front stable door stood two buckets planted with hemlock and night-shade. The top half of the door was open, and Divine's voice carried clearly out into the night air.

"I've waited *forever* to get my hooves on Queen Moonshine's special tiara. The pink rose quartz crystals look stunning against my dark coat, don't you think?" Divine gave a short laugh. "Queen Divine. It won't be long. Now that I have the castle jewels, I can claim my rightful place as ruler of Chevalia."

"You look wonderful, my lady," a rough voice agreed.

"Perfectly *divine*," chortled someone else. "Now, what about our payment?"

"Oh, that," she said. "Once I'm living at Stableside Castle as Queen of Chevalia, then you two farmhands shall have everything you ever dreamed of. Now, off you go, and don't tell anyone about tonight. I will summon you when I am able to reward you properly."

"Thank you, Ma'am, or should we say *your royal highness*?"

The stable door opened and Lanky and Hairy backed out, bowing to Divine as they left. Outside, they high-hooved each other before galloping away into the night.

"Pah!" Divine was talking to herself.

"Common farm ponies! They may have brought me the jewels, but that's where their glory ends. They should be grateful I let them help me." She chortled wickedly.

Mucker was outraged. "Common farm ponies! Divine needs reminding who provides her food. There'd be none of her favorite honeyed oat cakes if it wasn't for a *common* farmer!" he spat.

Pippa leaned over and put a hand on his mane. "Wait," she whispered. "I've got a better idea. Let's give her a fright, the same way she scared the royal family."

"Now, that's a plan," Stardust agreed.

Pippa slid from Stardust's back. "On the count of three," she whispered. "One, two, three—howl!"

The three friends opened their

mouths as wide as they could and shrieked like ghosts.

"Whooooooooo!"

The fearful sound ripped round the cottage and in through the door, growing louder and more ghostly as the jack-o'-lantern ghosts got into their role. Over the howls came the stomp of hooves. Divine peered into the night, snorting crossly.

"Hairy, Lanky! Stop making that noise."

Pippa, Stardust, and Mucker shared a grin as they continued to moan. "Whooooooooo!"

"Enough. That's an appalling racket." Divine stood in the doorway and glared into the night. "Stop it right now!"

"Whooooooooo!" Pippa was giggling

so much that it was hard to keep howling. She took a deep breath, and when she felt more composed she let rip with the loudest howl ever.

Divine's eyes bulged with fury as she stepped into the doorway. "Didn't you hear me? I said . . ."

Suddenly, Divine spotted the pumpkin ghosts.

The color drained from her face. A second later, she reared up, almost banging her head on the doorframe. "G . . . g . . . ghosts!"

With a shriek, Divine bolted outside. Kicking out her hooves, she galloped away into the forest.

Stardust started to cheer.

"Listen!" said Pippa, silencing her with a hand.

As Divine disappeared, there was a clatter of something falling.

"The jewels!"

Pippa, Stardust, and Mucker ran to pick up the castle jewels that had fallen from Divine as she bolted away.

"There's far too much to carry," said Stardust.

Pippa pulled off her pumpkin head.

"Phew!" she gasped. "That was hot and heavy. Worth it, though, because we can use our pumpkins as buckets!"

"You never stop amazing me, Pippa MacDonald!" Stardust's eyes shone with excitement as she removed her pumpkin.

They filled the hollowed-out pumpkins to the brim with jewels, searching the cottage carefully to make sure they'd gotten everything. Pippa loaded the pumpkins onto Stardust and Mucker's backs.

It was a long trek through the Wild Forest, and there were lots of mysterious squeaks coming from the bushes. But the trio felt full of courage and trekked onwards. After a while, Stardust stopped. "Did you hear that?" she whinnied.

"Yes." Pippa drew up next to her and Mucker. "Someone's howling. It sounds more like a pony than a ghost, though."

Pony hooves thundered closer, and a group of Wild Ponies appeared, carrying straw bags around their necks. "Whoooo!" they shrieked. "Happy Halloween!"

"Happy Halloween," Pippa, Stardust, and Mucker called back.

"That looks like fun," said Pippa longingly.

"If we hurry, then there'll be time to go trick-or-treating when we get back," said Stardust.

Stardust set off at a smart trot with Pippa and Mucker jogging alongside, until they reached the plateau and Mane Street. The town was packed with small ponies dressed up as ghosts, witches, and, to Pippa's delight, zonies, all out trick-or-treating with their parents. They stopped, staring as Pippa and her pony friends clattered along Mane Street carrying the royal jewels. Some of the ponies followed behind, and by the time they reached the royal camp, the friends were leading a large procession.

"Look!" cried Comet, who'd been reading by torchlight outside his tent, "The royal jewels."

"The royal jewels!" A cry went up, and all the royal ponies rushed outside to cheer Pippa, Stardust, and Mucker home.

"What's all the noise about?" asked Queen Moonshine, coming out of a tent with King Firestar.

Quickly, Pippa explained how Divine had stolen the royal jewels by pretending that Stableside Castle was haunted.

"Outrageous," said King Firestar, shaking his copper-colored head. "You were right, my dear Queen. We should have remained where we were instead of feeling forced to leave our home.

Next time I'll listen to you and not the courtiers."

Queen Moonshine smiled graciously. "We will all be wiser next time. But for now, we must thank these brave young heroes. Once again, they have saved us from Divine's mean tricks. Thank you, Pippa. Thank you, Mucker and Stardust."

"It was fun," said Pippa. Then she blushed furiously when everyone burst out laughing. "It *was* fun!" she insisted.

"And now we can return to the castle, just in time for the Halloween Feast," said the Queen. "I hope you will join us, Pippa. There'll be dancing, games, and lots of lovely food. There's a competition for the scariest pony and lots of tricks and treats. And this year, in your honor, I'm going to start a new tradition of giving every pony a chocolate-dipped carrot." Queen Moonshine paused, her dark eyes on Pippa's as she waited for an answer.

"That sounds lovely," said Pippa wistfully. "Maybe I could stay for a little while, but not too long. I want to go home to finish trick-or-treating with my own family."

"Of course." Queen Moonshine nodded in understanding. Tapping a hoof on the ground, she called, "Courtiers, take the jewels back to the castle. Ponies of Chevalia, please join us for the Halloween Feast."

"Hurrah!" roared the crowd.

Chapter 8

Pippa leaned against a rough stone wall as she took in the splendor of the ballroom. Flying bats and cobwebs decorated with colored spiders hung from the ceiling. The room was lit by the orange glow of a thousand flickering jack-o'-lanterns. At one end of the room, horse troughs were filled to overflowing with Halloween treats such as pumpkin pie, spider mash, hot bat punch, chocolate-dipped carrots,

and, especially for Pippa, pumpkin pizza.

"I'm so happy that Farmer Squash and Marrow won the prize for the biggest jack-o'-lantern, even though this year their enormous pumpkins won't make it to the Harvest Fair," said Pippa.

She glanced over at the two pumpkin heads discarded by Hairy and Lanky. Queen Moonshine had ordered that the pumpkins be turned into giant jack-o-lanterns. Farmer Squash and Marrow posed proudly with their giant pumpkins for photos, happily showing off the results of their farming while boasting that next year the pumpkins would be even bigger.

"Me too," Stardust sighed. "I'm so

full, but I can't resist those chocolate-dipped carrots. Do you want one?"

"Nooo!" groaned Pippa. Her stomach felt as if it might burst.

"I do," said Princess Crystal, who was passing. "They're the nicest . . ." Her eyes widened and her nostrils flared. "Eeek!" she shrieked, waving her front hooves. "A ghost!"

"Wait, Princess Crystal. It's only me." Cloud swooped into the ballroom and hovered in front of Pippa. She chuckled. "Although I'm getting used to ponies calling me a ghost! I've come to take Pippa home."

Stardust hung her head sadly. "Does she have to go back right now?"

Pippa nodded. "I'd love to stay for

longer, but I should be out trick-or-treating with my family. It's our tradition."

"Family is important," said Queen Moonshine.

Princess Stardust gave Pippa the longest hug ever before letting her go. Next, Pippa said good-bye to Queen Moonshine, King Firestar, and all her Chevalia pony friends. Finally, after pulling on her zony hood again, Pippa climbed onto Cloud's back. "Good-bye, Stardust. See you soon."

Pippa waved until Stardust and then the island were tiny specks on the horizon. Then she snuggled down on Cloud's back, with her head resting against the pony's soft neck.

Cloud flew steadily on, and in hardly

any time at all Pippa saw her home drawing closer.

"Hold tight," Cloud whinnied, her huge wings beating rhythmically as she flew down toward Pippa's road.

Pippa smiled at her family, who were still frozen in exactly the same poses as when she'd left them. It was almost as if she'd never been away.

"'Bye, Cloud," she said, sliding from her back.

"Goodbye, Pippa. See you again soon."

As Pippa touched the ground, her family came to life again. Miranda pounced on her.

"Scaredy-cat," she said. "I dare you to trick-or-treat at the haunted house."

Pippa smiled. If only Miranda knew about the ghostly frights she'd had in

Chevalia! They made the house at the end of her street look tame. "All right," she agreed.

"Really?" Miranda's mouth fell open. "Pippa, wait," she said, chasing her sister along the street. "I didn't mean it . . ."

But Pippa was already marching through the overgrown garden and up to the door. Up close, Pippa decided the house looked more neglected than haunted. The windows were dirty, the paintwork was peeling, and crisp brown leaves littered the doorstep. The doorbell was broken, so Pippa knocked on the door.

It was ages before anyone answered. Pippa almost gave up, thinking the house was empty, but then she heard a thumping and footsteps coming closer. The door swung open, and an elderly lady with long gray hair wound into a bun, gold eyeglasses, and a walking stick peered out. "Can I help you?" croaked Mrs. Parsons, her hand trembling.

Mrs. MacDonald, Miranda, and Jack came up behind Pippa as she was saying, "Happy Halloween! Trick or treat?"

"I'm sorry, my dear," Mrs. Parsons

said sadly, "but I haven't been able to get out to the stores. That's why I didn't leave my porch light on. I was so scared I'd upset you kids because I don't have any candy to give away."

"Don't be scared," said Pippa, remembering how the pumpkin ghost had frightened the royal family and how Cloud had terrified the farmers. "Things aren't always as they seem. We can go shopping for you, can't we, Mom?" Pippa turned to her mother.

"Of course we can," said Mrs. Mac-Donald. "I'll come by tomorrow morning, and you can give me a list."

"That's very kind. I'll be sure to put candy on it. I'm sorry I don't have anything to give you kids now, though. Your costumes are great. The zony and skeleton are very scary. And, I hope you don't mind me saying," she paused and studied Miranda, "you make a very glamorous witch."

Miranda blushed, but Pippa could tell she was pleased.

Impulsively, Pippa reached into her candy bucket and handed some to Mrs. Parsons. "Here, this is for you. We've got plenty."

"Why, thank you." Mrs. Parsons's eyes crinkled as she smiled at Pippa. "You kids must come round tomorrow, too. I'll get your mom to buy some cookies, and you can stay for a morning snack."

"That sounds awesome," said Pippa.

"Yay for Halloween!" added Jack.

"Halloween's silly," said Miranda as they finally made their way home, but her eyes sparkled in the light of the full moon.

"Does that mean you don't want your candy?" asked Pippa innocently.

"I never said that," said Miranda quickly.

Pippa smiled. "This has been the best Halloween," she said, "because we spent it together."

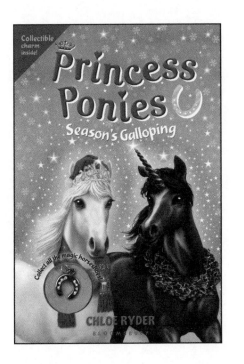

Hidden in the middle of the seas is the island of Chevalia, a magical place surrounded by golden beaches. It's ruled by the royal ponies Queen Moonshine and King Firestar from their court at Stableside Castle.

But a long way from Stableside, in the middle of the Horseshoe Hills, was a smaller, dilapidated castle with crumbling ivy-clad walls. Mice and beetles lived in the empty rooms. Bats roosted in the turrets and spiders hung from thick webs.

In a dark room with spots of damp peppering the walls, a mean-looking pony with a square nose was preparing to go out. She put on a black cloak and pulled the hood over her face. Next, she covered her hooves with foam-backed horseshoes. The pony, whose name was Divine, walked to the opposite side of the room, then trotted back. Her hooves made no sound on the stone floor.

"Perfect!" A wicked smile lit Divine's face. "No one will hear me when I walk down Mane Street to strip the Christmas tree of its decorations."

Reaching up, Divine unhooked a large sack from a nail on the wall. She hung it round her neck and went out through the back door. On silent hooves, Divine galloped to Mane Street.

While the ponies of Chevalia slept, Divine stared at the enormous Christmas tree, tall and proud at the end of the street. Its snowy branches were covered with horseshoe decorations that sparkled in the moonlight. Divine set to work, removing the horseshoes and hiding them in her sack. When the tree was empty, she brushed the stray pine needles and glitter from her cloak. A wicked smile lit her sallow face.

"Chevalia," she whispered, "I've ruined Christmas for you. Only when you accept me as your rightful queen will I stop thinking up ways to make your lives as miserable as mine."

Divine cackled softly as she galloped away, the tree decorations bouncing in her sack.

Pippa MacDonald woke early. It was unnaturally quiet, and the room was bathed in a bright white light. Butterflies danced in her stomach as she leapt out of bed.

"Snow!" Pippa's breath came out in a white cloud as she threw back the curtains and stared onto the street. "Snow for Christmas day."

On tiptoes, Pippa crept downstairs

to the Christmas tree. The fresh smell of pine needles tickled her nose.

"Wow!" she gasped. The tree stood in a sea of presents. Pippa's eyes traveled over the parcels, trying to guess the contents from their shape. So many of the gift tags had her name written on them, but had she gotten the present she wanted the most? "Please let there be ice skates!" Pippa had her heart set on a white pair that she'd seen in Tillingdale's department store.

Pippa couldn't wait for her family, Mom, Miranda, and Jack, to wake so she could find out.

Jack woke next. He ran around the tree shouting, "Choo choo!" He'd been hoping for a train set.

Miranda clumped down the stairs, grumbling. "Why so loud?"

"It's Christmas!" Pippa squealed.

"Presents, presents, presents!" Jack yelled as their Mom followed them into the front room.

"Can we open them now?" asked Pippa hopefully.

"Not yet," said Mom, her face serious. "There's been a change of plan. We're going to school."

"Good one!" Pippa laughed, thinking that her mother was joking. No one went to school on Christmas morning.

"It's true," said Mom.

"Ha ha ha!" Jack giggled.

"I'm sorry, kids, but a friend called me late last night. She's using the school kitchens and gym to prepare a Christmas feast for local people who aren't as lucky as we are. But she doesn't have enough helpers, so I said we'd go along too.

"Really? Suddenly I don't feel so lucky," said Miranda.

"I'm not going to school on Christmas day!" Jack jumped up and down. "No!" he shouted. "No. No. No."

"Yes," said Mom firmly. "We can all help out. And our Christmas can wait for a few more hours."

Pippa frowned. She didn't want to help either. But it seemed mean not to, especially when Christmas was supposed to be a time of good will.

After a hurried breakfast, they wrapped up in warm coats and winter boots. Jack was still being difficult, so Pippa volunteered to pull him on a sled. Mom was carrying two large bags filled with food.

"Why don't you pop them on the sled, Mom?" offered Pippa. "I can pull the groceries and the brother!"

Mom placed the bags in between Jack's legs and said, "Hold on to these."

"I'll eat it all up," he joked with a smile.

As they trudged through the snow on the familiar route toward school, Pippa pretended she was a reindeer pulling Santa's sleigh across the sky. But of course it was much harder to walk in the snow than fly through the air.

Still, Pippa loved hearing the crunch of the snow as her feet sank into it and seeing how the sled's train smoothed over her footprints as she pulled it. As they neared the school, they joined up with other parents and children. Many of them were also carrying bags of food.

"Cody!" called Pippa, catching sight of her best friend. She hurried across the yard and caught up to Cody by the frozen duck pond next to the gym. "Merry Christmas."

"Right back at ya," said Cody. She

pointed to a pair of ducks huddled together at the edge of the pond. "Look at them, poor things. The ice is so thick they've got nowhere to swim."

"They'll have to learn to ice skate," said Pippa. Her heart leaped with wonder. Had she gotten the ice skates she wanted?

The gym was buzzing with activity. Volunteers of all ages, wearing Santa

hats, were busy hanging decorations and setting the tables. In the school's kitchen, which joined onto the gym, a group of parents was singing as they prepared the Christmas feast.

"Mmm," said Pippa, her stomach rumbling in appreciation. "Something smells delicious."

"There's no time for daydreaming." Mom came up behind Pippa. "We've got a ton of work to do to make this day special."

"Yes, ma'am!" said Pippa smartly. She gave Mom a mock salute. "What can I do first?"

"Open the door," said Mom. She pushed her brown hair away from her face. "It's getting hot in here."

Pippa ran to the door and opened it

wide. A flurry of fresh snow rushed in on a cold breeze. Pippa opened her mouth to catch the snowflakes on her tongue. Most of them landed on her nose, making her giggle. Out of the corner of her eye, Pippa saw something gliding closer. She stopped catching snowflakes and stared in surprise.

It was a pony. A pony with wings.

"Princess Cloud?" Pippa blinked and rubbed her eyes. "Is it really you?"

Pippa couldn't believe that Princess Cloud would be here on Christmas day, but the ponies of Chevalia always found ways to surprise her.

Princess Cloud flew across the yard and hovered in front of her.

"Hello, Pippa," she said breathlessly. "I'm so glad I've found you at last!"